Text by Daniel Mauleón
Illustrated by Fran Bueno

STONE ARCH BOOKS
a capstone imprint

Published by Stone Arch Books, an imprint of Capstone.
1710 Roe Crest Drive North Mankato, Minnesota 56003
capstonepub.com

Library of Congress Cataloging-in-Publication Data
Names: Maddox, Jake, author. | Mauleón, Daniel, 1991–
    author. | Bueno Capeáns, Francisco, illustrator.
Title: Jungle mastermind / Jake Maddox ; by Daniel
    Mauleón ; illustrated by Francisco Bueno Capeáns.
Description: North Mankato, Minnesota : Stone Arch
    Books, 2022. | Series: Jake Maddox esports | Audience:
    Ages 8-12. | Audience: Grades 4-6.
Summary: Antonia volunteers to play a different role
    when a new and inexperienced player joins her esports
    team, but when her new position proves to be more
    difficult than she expected, she realizes she must learn
    new strategies or risk letting her team down.
Identifiers: LCCN 2021056949 (print) | LCCN 2021056950
    (ebook) | ISBN 9781666344608 (hardcover) | ISBN
    9781666353310 (paperback) | ISBN 9781666344646 (pdf)
Subjects: LCSH: eSports (Contests)--Juvenile fiction. |
    Teamwork (Sports)—Juvenile fiction. | Self-confidence—
    Juvenile fiction. | Friendship—Juvenile fiction. | CYAC:
    eSports (Contests)—Fiction. | Teamwork (Sports—-Fiction. |
    Self-confidence--Fiction. | Friendship—Fiction.
Classification: LCC PZ7.M25643 Jun 2022 (print) | LCC PZ7.
    M25643 (ebook) | DDC 813.6 [Fic]—dc23/eng/20211223
LC record available at https://lccn.loc.gov/2021056949
LC ebook record available at https://lccn.loc.gov/2021056950

Editor: Aaron Sautter
Designers: Brann Garvey, Elyse White
Production Spe

Shutterstock: E
(pixel texture)

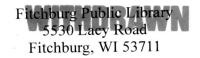

TABLE OF CONTENTS

THE HEROES OF
MOBIUS BRIDGE

THUNDER OWL
ROLE: JUNGLER

THE ELECTRO-WINGED WONDER!

+ Speed
- Defense

Basic Attack: Zap Feathers
Boosted Attack: Shocking Spin
Dash Attack: Dazzling Dash
Special Attack: Static Feathers

LUMINARY
ROLE: OFFENSE

*THE MUSCLED HERO
OF LUMINOUS CITY!*

+ Strength
- Health

Basic Attack: Powered Punch
Boosted Attack: Focus Beam
Dash Attack: Flying Dash
Special Attack: Luminous Slam

MECHA-KNIGHT
ROLE: DEFENDER

THE ROBOTIC SUIT OF ARMOR!

+ Defense
- Speed

Basic Attack: Slicing Sword
Boosted Attack: Spinning Sword
Dash Attack: Shield Bash
Special Attack: Mini-Missile Volley

CRASH
ROLE: JUNGLER

LIFEGUARD SURFER TURNED HERO!

+ Attack
- Defense

Basic Attack: Super Slash
Boosted Attack: Hydropunches
Dash Attack: Waverider
Special Attack: Power Preserver

CHAPTER 1

THE MOBIUS BRIDGE

Yesterday, in the skies above Luminous City, another Earth appeared. It arrived with a loud crack—as if space itself had been split open.

Everyone stopped what they were doing and stared up at this second Earth. It looked just like Earth, but it glowed orange. Then the ground began to rumble, and around the city five huge pillars emerged and rose into the clouds. They looked like perfectly round skyscrapers made of metal and glass. The pillars grew until they reached into space.

Within minutes, a team of Earth's greatest superheroes climbed the pillars into space. But halfway up, they made a shocking discovery.

They felt the gravity shift, and they "fell up" the pillars toward the sky. When the heroes landed with a thud, they stood up and looked around. They were on a city floating in space between the two planets. Looking down the street, the heroes noticed something very odd. The city flipped in the middle like a thin strip of paper twisted around on itself.

"Where are we?" asked Luminary.

The muscled champion of Luminous City looked up at the pillars they had just climbed. Above her, she could see her Earth. Luminary always knew the planet was blue. But from space, it seemed to have a vibrant blue glow. In fact, she also seemed to be glowing blue.

"Welcome to the Mobius Bridge," said a familiar voice—too familiar.

A figure stepped out from behind a building. She had big broad muscles, a cape, and a loose curl of hair poking from behind an orange mask.

The figure looked just like Luminary. Wait . . . no, this was a Luminary from the Orange Earth! And she glowed orange just like her own planet.

The copycat spoke again, "Now get out of our way."

A team of orange heroes, just like the blue ones from Earth, soon appeared. They looked ready to fight. The Orange Luminary continued, "Only one Earth can survive. We're going to destroy your pillars and, with it, your planet."

*   *   *

Luminary flew through the streets of the Mobius Bridge. Running beside her was another hero: The Outstanding Ox. He was a giant ox who stood on two feet and had a devastating hoof punch. The battle with the Orange Earth heroes had gone on for over a day. Blue Earth's team had destroyed three of the enemies' pillars. If they took out the last two, their home would be safe.

The ground under Luminary began to twist. They were entering the underside of the Mobius Bridge. Soon, the Orange Earth floated above their heads. Just thinking about the twisting streets and changing gravity made Luminary dizzy.

"There it is!" Ox shouted.

He got down on all four limbs and charged toward an enemy pillar. Luminary summoned a boost of strength and zipped forward. She slammed into the pillar with her mighty strength, and . . .

CRACK!

Ox then punched with his powerful left hoof, then his right, into the towering structure. It cracked some more. The pillar began to flash in alarm.

Secret panels opened on its sides. From these panels popped little turrets, which shot laser blasts at the two heroes. Next, two large doors opened at the bottom of the pillar and small robot minions marched out.

Luminary and her team had learned the hard way that the pillars weren't defenseless. But once they knew what to expect, it wasn't much of a challenge.

Ox puffed up his chest and roared. This drew the attention of the turrets, which began firing at him. The blasts sizzled on his blue hide. "Ha, ha!" Ox chuckled. "Your wimpy lasers are nothing against my tough skin."

Meanwhile, Luminary gathered energy in her hands. They began to glow. Then she directed the energy out in a focused beam to knock out the turrets. In less than a minute, the two heroes had turned the bots and turrets to scrap. Luminary turned back to the pillar and continued pounding it with her powerful fists.

"Go on ahead, Ox," Luminary shouted. "I'll finish this pillar."

Ox grunted in agreement. Then he got on all fours and sprinted down the street.

Luminary got back to work smashing the pillar. But after a few seconds she heard a scream for help. It was Ox. If he needed help, that could only mean one thing.

LUMINARY

CHAPTER 2

ANTONIA

Antonia looked from her computer monitor over to her friend sitting next to her. "You okay, Paul?"

Usually, Antonia would play *Mobius Bridge* in the comfort of her bedroom. But she was currently in the school's computer lab playing with Paul and Amanda. They were part of the school's esports team. Practice was supposed to have started twenty minutes ago, but their captain was running late. So the three players had joined an online quick match and were paired with two random online players.

"That was some great advice you had sending me ahead!" Paul said sarcastically. He was frantically tapping on his keyboard with one hand while the other whipped his mouse around.

Antonia laughed, "I'll be right there. Let me finish this pillar!"

Antonia looked back at her screen. *Mobius Bridge* was played in a top-down view. Antonia saw her character, Luminary, from above. She was still fighting the pillar. She tapped a key on her keyboard to select Luminary's Focus Beam. On-screen, Luminary blasted down the pillar with her powerful ability. As it came down, the screen flashed a message: *One Pillar Left!*

"Antonia," Paul said, worried.

"Coming!" Antonia responded and navigated Luminary to the right of the screen.

Mobius Bridge was a MOBA, a Multiplayer Online Battle Arena game. Like other MOBAs, the map was split into multiple lanes. *Mobius Bridge* had a top lane, a bottom lane, and a Jungle in the middle. Two teams of five duked it out across these lanes.

Antonia and Paul were playing the top lane. It was designed like a dense city, with skyscrapers and streets. The bottom lane was guarded by Amanda and an online player. Another online player guarded the Jungle.

After a few moments, Antonia saw what Paul was worried about. On her screen, Luminary caught up to Ox at the final pillar for Orange Earth. But he wasn't alone. Four of the enemy heroes were also there, including another Luminary.

"A 2 v 4? I don't think I like these odds," Antonia said.

"Let's even it out," Amanda said. Soon Luminary and Ox were joined by their two allies from the bottom lane.

Now this is a proper fight! Antonia thought.

Each hero in *Mobius Bridge* had unique moves. Antonia knew Luminary's abilities like the back of her hand. With the tap of a key, she activated Luminary's flying dash and dove into combat. She followed that up with some basic punches. On-screen, Luminary pummeled her enemies.

POW! BAM! CRUNCH!

Antonia pressed another key, activating Luminary's Focus Beam. Then she spun her mouse, making Luminary spin in a circle to slice through nearby enemies. Finally, Antonia tapped another key to activate Luminary's special move, Luminous Slam. She flew into the air, gathered all her energy and crashed back to the ground. The impact created a devastating explosion.

Battling together, Antonia's team crushed their enemies, sending them back to their home pillar. It would be thirty seconds before they respawned, giving her team time to take out the last pillar. By the time the enemy team returned, it was too late.

"Woohoo!" Amanda shouted, pumping her fist.

"See, Paul, it wasn't a problem at all," Antonia said.

Paul still looked stressed. "Speak for yourself. That was too close for my comfort."

"Great job, everyone!" came a voice from behind them.

It was Tommy, the team captain. Next to Tommy stood a shy girl. Antonia smiled at her and waved. The girl gave a small wave back before looking away.

Tommy spoke again, "Everyone, meet our newest teammate, Maria."

CHAPTER 3

CHANGING LANES

Tommy and Maria pulled up a couple of chairs as the others spun around in theirs.

"As you know, our season starts in two weeks and we were still looking for a fifth player to take the Jungle." Tommy said. "Well, I found our fifth player. However, Maria isn't used to the Jungle. It would help if she didn't have to learn a new role while learning to play with us at the same time."

"What role do you play, Maria?" Paul asked. *Mobius Bridge* had five general roles. The top lane had an Offensive Hero and a Defensive hero. Both were usually great at close-quarters combat. The bottom lane had an Attacker and a Supporter. The Attacker was a powerful hero but needed balance from the Supporter to last long in battle.

Then there was the middle lane, also known as the Jungle, which had a unique role called the Jungler. These heroes moved quickly and had deadly attacks. But they lacked strength and defenses. Because of their location in the middle of the map, they could join fights in the other lanes and tip the battle.

"Umm," Maria paused, "I'm usually in the top lane, playing Offense."

Offense was Antonia's role. But Tommy spoke before she could say anything.

"I don't want to push anyone off their role. But we need someone to play the Jungler."

"I'll do it," Antonia said before thinking. Just like Luminary, Antonia enjoyed coming to the rescue. But would she really want to switch roles?

"I can switch to support and join Amanda on the bottom lane," Paul said to Tommy. "That way, you and Maria can play the top lane together."

"Sounds like a plan!" Tommy said. "Take some time and look over your hero choices. I want to catch Maria up on some of our strategies."

Mobius Bridge added a few new heroes each year. The game had been out for several years, so there were a lot of heroes to pick from in each role.

Junglers all had low hit points but made up for it in two ways. First, they were very mobile. They could move around the map quickly, weaving in and out of obstacles and enemies. Second, they had some of the most powerful moves in the game.

Antonia stared at the character select screen. There were dozens of Junglers to choose from. Antonia went one by one,

looking over and comparing their different profiles. She didn't care much about the heroes' biographies and backgrounds. Instead, she skipped straight to their various powers and abilities.

After skimming through a few screens, one of the heroes caught Antonia's eye. It was a woman with white and black wings.

The hero's super suit was black with yellow and blue trim. Every few seconds, a bolt of blue electricity would travel across her body, and her eyes would glow white.

Now this is my kind of hero. Antonia smiled as she selected Thunder Owl.

CHAPTER 4

WELCOME TO THE JUNGLE

"Okay, listen up, everyone," Tommy said to the room. Antonia pulled her attention from her monitor. She had spent the last twenty minutes in a training room practicing Thunder Owl's moves.

Once Tommy had everyone's attention, he continued. "I scheduled a scrimmage today against East High. We have an uphill fight with a new teammate and new roles. However, it'll give us a good chance to see where we need to improve."

Antonia already missed playing as Luminary. With Luminary, she knew the best order to chain her abilities together to KO minions and other players. Then there was the map. Antonia didn't know where and when the Jungle minions would spawn. Since defeating minions was the best way to level up, she would struggle with that too.

As the scrimmage started, Antonia and her teammates spawned at their home pillar on the far left of the map. Amanda and Paul headed to the bottom lane. Tommy and Maria went to the top lane.

Meanwhile, Antonia ran straight forward into the Jungle. The Jungle in this game was an old city park full of thick weeds and big, overgrown trees. A big open field in the park was tangled with thick vines and bushes.

Thunder Owl flew just a bit off the ground. As she made her way through the Jungle, the first minions spawned. The Jungle minions were various beasts and monsters. One was a large mutant frog with bumpy green skin and purple eyes.

MUTANT FROG

THUNDER OWL

As the frog faced Thunder Owl, it spat toxic bubbles that landed with a *POP!* This was a small minion, so it didn't do much damage.

Antonia clicked her mouse to counter. Thunder Owl flapped her wings and sent a bolt of electricity at the frog. Antonia kept clicking. Each click created another bolt of lightning and the frog soon fell, giving Thunder Owl some experience.

Antonia felt a thrill from taking down the frog. With a few more minions like that, Thunder Owl could level up, gain more health, and increase her attack and defense stats. She could even learn some new moves with some level ups. Antonia continued through the Jungle in search of more minions.

Before long, Thunder Owl had cleared the minions from her side of the Jungle and had learned a new move: Shocking Spin.

This might be enough to take on the enemy Jungler, Antonia thought. She navigated

Thunder Owl to head right on the map, to the enemy's side of the Jungle.

In the middle of the Jungle was a park plaza. Although it was overgrown with plants, it was still an open space, with a large fountain in the middle. But in the fountain was a giant mutant squirrel!

Thunder Owl went in for the kill, but before she could get close, a sudden wave came smashing down from the right. On top of the wave was Crash, a lifeguard surfer turned superhero. It was the Orange Earth's Jungler. The wave first took out the squirrel and then crashed into Thunder Owl. The impact wasn't enough to KO Antonia, but it hurt.

Thunder Owl was dazed for a moment, but then recovered. She stood up and waited for Crash to be in range. When he got close, she activated her ability: Shocking Spin. Thunder Owl spun in a circle and her wings sent out waves of electricity.

The electricity zapped the surfing hero, but Crash fought back. He covered his fists in boxing gloves made from water. Then he unleashed a flurry of hydro-powered punches.

POW! BAM! CRUNCH! KO!

Before she knew it, Thunder Owl was sent back to respawn.

Antonia was stunned. She knew Junglers didn't have much health. But she was taken out much quicker than she expected.

After ten seconds, Thunder Owl respawned by the home pillar. Antonia shook off the fight. It was silly to think she would win her first fight with a new character.

Thunder Owl headed back into the Jungle. By now, the mutant minions there had also respawned. Antonia worked to clear them out again. When she had dusted some frogs and a few mutant squirrels, she had reached level five and gained another new move: Dazzling Dash.

Antonia tried out her new power on an unsuspecting mutant frog. She held down the activation key to power up her new move. Then she moved her mouse to target the frog. On the screen, Thunder Owl dashed toward the frog with lightning trailing behind her. She collided with the frog with a bright flash and a thunderclap. The frog was toast.

Now that's cool!

"Argh! Help!" came a voice over the team chat. During the game the other players chatted about what they were doing in their lanes. For the most part, Antonia tuned it out. Her role in the Jungle was a lonely one.

"Oh no," the voice said worriedly. It was Maria.

Antonia quickly headed toward the top lane to join Maria and Tommy. She just hoped she could get there in time.

CHAPTER 5

DISASTER ON MOBIUS BRIDGE

Near the edge of the Jungle, an incredible battle continued. Two heroes of Blue Earth, Luminary and Mecha-Knight, faced off against their Orange Earth equals.

Blue Luminary gathered energy, took aim, and blasted it at the Orange Mecha-Knight. The Mecha-Knight was a medieval suit of armor turned into a battling robot. Luminary's blue beam grazed the Orange Knight, but the armor held steady.

Then the Orange Knight slammed its shield into the Blue Mecha-Knight. The Blue Knight stumbled backward into a powerful punch from the Orange Luminary. It was a well-timed combo.

The Blue Heroes were on the ropes. But suddenly, another hero burst on the scene.

BLUE LUMINARY

BLUE MECHA-KNIGHT

THUNDER OWL

ORANGE MECHA-KNIGHT

ORANGE LUMINARY

Out of the sky, Thunder Owl dashed forward. She collided with the Orange heroes, doling out big damage. Thunder Owl whirled in place, shooting electricity in waves from her wings. For a moment, the Orange heroes were in trouble.

But then things changed quickly. The Orange Knight raised its shield and slammed it into Thunder Owl, stunning her in place. Then Orange Luminary leaped into the air and shot back to the ground with a huge quake attack. Still stunned by the shield, Thunder Owl couldn't move.

SMASH!

The Orange Luminary's devastating blow took out Thunder Owl.

* * *

"What?" Antonia shouted in the computer lab. That combo felt unfair.

"Oh no," Antonia added as she waited for the respawn.

While minions gave a little experience toward leveling up, knocking out a hero provided a lot more. By knocking out Thunder Owl with a combined attack, both Orange Heroes leveled up. Although the fight was an even 2 v 2, Tommy and Maria were behind in levels.

Antonia wanted to cover her eyes. First, Tommy was taken out by another combo. This left Maria's Luminary to fend for herself. She tried to safely retreat but was caught by one of Orange Luminary's beams.

"Sorry guys," Maria said into her mic.

"No, that's on me," Antonia said. "I jumped in and only powered them up."

"Don't worry about it," Tommy said. "Losses happen. Shake it off, and let's get back in there."

All three heroes spawned at the Home Pillar around the same time. Antonia thought about returning to the Jungle. She could try to level up on her own and hopefully be more help.

But Tommy and Maria would still be out-leveled in their lane. And that was her fault. Instead, Antonia directed Thunder Owl to follow Tommy and Maria to the top lane.

A few moments later, Antonia and the others faced the Orange enemy duo near the base of a blue pillar. Antonia tried her dash and spin combo again.

But she still wasn't used to Thunder Owl's keys. Instead of hitting the enemy, she spun too soon and sent the electric waves at nobody. She tried a dash attack next, but she was defenseless.

Antonia sighed. She knew what came next. The Orange team did a shield bash and focus beam combo, sending Thunder Owl back to respawn again.

Antonia needed to change things up. She brought up a stats screen. It showed the level of all the players in the match. She was at Level 5. The enemy was already Level 7.

It made sense. Antonia had lost her last two fights without killing any minions in between. Meanwhile, Crash had spent the last five minutes leveling up. Even worse, the top lane enemies were up to Level 8.

All thanks to me, she thought.

Antonia headed back into the Jungle. She cleaned out a few camps of mutant minions and was soon up to Level 7.

Things were looking up when Antonia heard the sound effect of rushing water. Here came the enemy Jungler. Antonia refocused. She felt she could take Crash one-on-one. After all, she had just leveled up twice. But when she rechecked the stats screen, her heart sank. While she had moved up to Level 7, Crash was now Level 9!

Before Antonia could react, Crash was stringing together a dangerous combo. He rode in on a wave and smacked Thunder Owl backwards. Then came the water fists. Antonia expected this and dashed out of the way of the punches. Then she slammed the key to activate her Shocking Spin.

But while Thunder Owl spun, Crash took aim. He tossed out a life preserver that caught Thunder Owl by surprise and pulled her in close. Then SPLASH! The preserver exploded in a powerful blast of water that took most of Thunder Owl's health.

Thunder Owl was low on hit points. Antonia knew this was a losing battle. But if she could get away and heal, maybe she could prevent Crash from leveling up.

A moment later, Thunder Owl's dash was recharged and ready to use. Antonia tapped the key and Thunder Owl followed the command, quickly boosting away from Crash.

"Yes!" Antonia exclaimed. But then, "Oh no."

Crash's wave-riding ability had recharged to cut off her escape. There was no hope. Her opponent knew their hero character better. Maybe after months of practice, Antonia could win a 1 v 1 match like this. But not today.

The surfing hero summoned another wave, which slammed into Thunder Owl and sent her to a watery grave. Antonia buried her face in her hands. Each respawn took longer and longer. That meant less time to level up and less time to help her team.

The rest of the game played out how Antonia feared. Whether she was helping in the top lane, or at the bottom, she kept getting in the way. If she spent too long in the Jungle, Crash would come to find her for a quick KO. It was a disaster. Thankfully, it didn't last long. The enemy team had soon destroyed all five of the Blue Team's pillars and won the match.

CHAPTER 6

PITY PARTY PEP TALK

Antonia got up and walked straight outside. She needed fresh air. As she sat on the school steps, she heard the door creak open behind her. She didn't turn around.

"You okay?" It was Tommy. Antonia scooted over to make room and thought about how to answer.

She took in a deep breath. "No," she said. "I'm not."

"Antonia, you did well for your first time as a Jungler," Tommy said, trying his best to comfort her.

"Yeah, maybe. But I expected better from myself," she responded. Antonia was used to being one of the best players on the team. She liked being reliable and helping her team. She didn't feel like she needed help herself.

"I get that," Tommy replied. "That's why I'm happy you volunteered to change roles. I know you'll do what it takes to learn the new hero. But you also have to take it easy on yourself."

"*Take it easy*?" Antonia burst out. "How can I take it easy when I can't do anything to help? I only made things worse for everyone."

Now it was Tommy's turn to think. "Okay. Bad choice of words. You're right. We need you to figure things out pretty quick. We've only got a couple of weeks until the season officially starts. But this was just your first game. Don't beat yourself up over it."

Antonia smiled. Tommy was a good captain. The "Take it Easy" speech would have worked great for Paul. But she preferred when Tommy was direct. That said, she wasn't sure she could pull it off.

"I've spent months playing top lane," Antonia responded. "How am I going to squish all of that experience into just a couple of weeks?"

"You won't," Tommy said bluntly. "But you can get started, and I can give you some tips. I've played a lot of the Jungle when I'm not playing with the team."

"Really?" Antonia asked.

"Yep," Tommy smiled. "Here's the thing about the Jungle. You need to be selfish. And you need to trust your team to take care of themselves."

Antonia didn't say anything. She just nodded.

"In today's game, you came rushing to help Maria and me," Tommy continued. "That's nice of you, but that was our fight to figure out."

"So I'm just supposed to stay in the Jungle the whole game?" Antonia was confused.

"Not exactly," Tommy said. "But you need to spend enough time there to level up to where you can take a few hits. Junglers like Thunder

42

Owl are glass cannons. You can deal a lot of damage, but you're also fragile. So, when you're ready, swoop in, deal your damage, and then get out. You may not get the KOs, but you can help turn the tide."

"But if I stay too long," Antonia continued, "then I can be a risk."

"Exactly," Tommy said. "It's all about the timing. One last thing, give it your all for a while, then we can revisit everyone's role. I don't want you to be stuck with something you don't want to play."

"Thanks, Tommy," Antonia flashed Tommy a smile as he went inside. Antonia thought about what he'd said. Be selfish. Trust your team. It was a bit confusing, but she thought she got it.

"I'm sorry," came another voice. Antonia jumped. She hadn't even heard the door open. She turned around to see Maria standing in the doorway.

CHAPTER 7

MEETING MARIA

"Sorry for what?" Antonia asked.

"What happened in the game. I'm new, and you had to change roles. And then we lost. When you left, I thought it was because of me."

Antonia couldn't help but laugh. She stood up and dusted herself off.

"No. I was mad at myself," she said. "You had nothing to do with it."

"Oh, okay," Maria said nervously. It was clear Maria was uneasy about being on a new team. For as worried as Antonia was about playing a new role, she wasn't alone.

"Look, I get it. Playing on a team is different than playing with random people online. But thankfully, we have a great team."

Antonia hoped she was as good at giving pep talks as Tommy. "Even though we had a bad game, we can learn to help each other out. In fact, I'm going to get in some extra practice this week. So if you want to get together for any matches, let me know. I could use the company."

Maria smiled. "Yes, please!"

Even if Antonia needed to be alone in the Jungle to level up, it didn't mean she had to be alone while she played. Antonia gave Maria a wide smile. "Great! Now let's head back in."

*   *   *

The next two weeks went by in a blur. Antonia spent all her free time practicing *Mobius Bridge*. Maria often joined her, and as they played, they would chat. They shared strategies and talked about other hobbies and interests. They both loved animals, bubble tea, and reading mystery novels.

Antonia memorized the layout of the Jungle. She learned how long it took for the minions to spawn, and the order they came in. First were the frogs, then the giant bugs, and finally the big squirrel in the fountain.

Antonia also figured out the best way to chain Thunder Owl's moves. She'd start with a Power Dash. Then after using her Shocking Spin and a few regular attacks, her Power Dash would be ready again. Depending on how the fight went, she'd dash away quickly or use it to finish knockouts. And of course, she learned how to use Thunder Owl's special move: Static Feathers.

When Antonia activated Static Feathers, the hero would point her wings at a target and blast it with electrically charged feathers. The static electricity would pull enemies in and deal a lot of damage. It also made them easy targets.

But even though Antonia felt more confident, she couldn't get that first scrimmage game out

of her mind. She remembered how many times she was knocked out, and how she had helped the other team level up.

So as the team gathered in the computer lab for their first official game of the season, Antonia forgot all about her training. Instead, she was just worried.

Tommy gave the team a speech about working together and doing their best. But Antonia couldn't focus. Suddenly, Maria nudged her.

"Hey, get out of your head. You've got this, Antonia," Maria said.

"Thanks," Antonia smiled in response as their team loaded into *Mobius Bridge*.

CHAPTER 8

THE GAME BEGINS

ZAP! FLAP! BOOM!

The mutant frogs in the Jungle didn't know what hit them. Thunder Owl flew between the trees and over the weedy walkways. She made quick work of the different mutant minion camps.

"Ha ha!" Antonia laughed to herself. She was making great time cleaning up her side of the Jungle. Next, she went to the fountain right as the oversized squirrel spawned.

"You're all mine," she said.

DASH! SPIN! ZZZAAP!

Thunder Owl landed devastating damage on the squirrel. The squirrel tried to leap

49

at her with its pointy buck teeth. But she blasted it with another jolt of electricity, and the squirrel was literal toast.

Taking out the squirrel let Thunder Owl level up again—and just in time. Across the plaza, the orange team's Jungler appeared. It was a hero called Wishing Star. She floated on a star-shaped glider and blasted enemies with cosmic rays.

Antonia brought up the stats screen. Thanks to her beating the mutant squirrel, she was a whole level above Wishing Star.

Bring it on, Antonia thought.

The two heroes battled it out over the fountain. Thunder Owl led with a shocking spin. Wishing Star countered with a pointy star shower attack. Thunder Owl used her Quick Dash to escape the stars and landed behind Wishing Star. Antonia clicked her mouse and sent a flurry of elemental attacks.

WISHING STAR

THUNDER OWL

After a few seconds, both heroes were low on health. But then both of Thunder Owl's moves were recharged.

DASH! SPIN! ZZAAP!

Wishing Star was sent back to spawn, and Thunder Owl was the queen of the Jungle.

With no one to challenge her, Thunder Owl made her way to the opponent's side of the Jungle and took out a few of the minions. Unfortunately, it wasn't enough to level up. Still, without any minions, it would be harder for Wishing Star to gain more experience.

Antonia checked her map. She was near Amanda's and Paul's heroes, who were fighting the other team on the bottom lane. Antonia moved Thunder Owl in that direction. From the Jungle, she watched her teammates battle it out as she waited for her abilities to recharge.

When Thunder Owl was ready, she dashed in and struck both enemies. Then she activated her Shocking Spin move. It landed but wasn't lethal. The opposing heroes focused their attacks on Thunder Owl, and she soon grew low on health.

Antonia decided to retreat and quickly dashed away to the comfort of the Jungle.

"Hope that helps," Antonia said over the mic to Amanda and Paul.

"It's perfect!" Paul said. "You've given us a huge opportunity."

Antonia watched from the Jungle's edge as her teammates KO'd the distracted and weakened enemies. Antonia thought about helping to fight the pillar. But she first had to retreat and heal.

Thunder Owl returned to heal up at the home pillar. Antonia could feel the smile growing on her face. There was still more to learn and a game to win. But she had learned to help her team in a whole new way.

CHAPTER 9

CAUGHT IN THE MIDDLE

The battle on the Mobius Bridge raged on. Although the Blue Earth team had an early lead, Orange Earth was catching up. After twenty minutes, both Earths had three pillars remaining. But in the heart of the Jungle, Antonia's Thunder Owl continued to grind.

As time went on, the minions in the Jungle grew stronger. The tiny mutant frogs now fought in packs. The bugs grew bigger and nastier. And the fountain was guarded by two more powerful squirrels.

But none of these bothered Antonia. This far into the game, she had found her rhythm in Thunder Owl's moves. She dashed in, unleashed a Spinning Shock and a few basic attacks, and then dashed away to reset.

Antonia checked the stats screen. She was still one level above the Orange Jungler. But she was still behind everyone else.

"HELP!" shouted Maria into her headset, "We're fighting three up here!"

"That explains where they went," Paul responded. "One of the bottom lane enemies went up top."

"I can head that way and help out. But it could take me a while to get there," said Amanda.

Antonia checked her map. She wasn't far from the fight. If she joined in, it would be a 3 v 3. But the enemies were higher level.

Would I help? Or would I just get in the way? Antonia thought to herself. *If the enemies KO me, they'll only get stronger and surely win.*

She spoke up, "I'm not ready. You'll have to wait for my help."

"That's okay," said Tommy. He was calm

and focused. "Maria, let's retreat carefully. If we can make it to our tower, that will give us extra protection. Paul and Amanda, stay where you are. Take advantage of your numbers in the bottom lane."

Antonia relaxed. Tommy was a great captain—both in and out of the game.

"That said," Tommy's voice came over comms again, "we'll likely need your help soon, Antonia."

"Okay! I'll be there as soon as I can," Antonia responded. Still looking at her map, she chose her path. On the way to the pillar, there would be two minion camps. Defeating both should give her enough experience to level up. But she would need to perfectly execute her combos if she wanted to be quick.

No time to keep thinking, Antonia thought. She closed her map and directed Thunder Owl through the Jungle.

CHAPTER 10

LIGHTNING STRIKES

Blue Luminary and Mecha-Knight had their backs against their pillar. Both were wounded badly. In front of them stood three heroes from the Orange Earth. They had arrived to finish the job. After they took out Luminary and Knight, they'd surely destroy the pillar.

"Dang," Luminary said. "We made it to the pillar, but I don't think we'll make it out alive."

"It was a good retreat," Mecha-Knight responded. "But sometimes it's not enough."

"Should we at least go out fighting?" Luminary asked. "My abilities are recharged."

"Wait," Mecha-Knight said, looking in the distance beyond the enemies. "Hold off until I say go."

The Orange Earth heroes laughed. It was easy pickings. But suddenly there was a flash of lightning. Bolts of electricity raced across the sky and struck the Orange Earth opponents. The attack knocked the trio over. They looked up to see who had hit them. Standing over them was Thunder Owl. Her wings were spread wide and they sizzled with energy.

*   *   *

Antonia slammed her special attack key. On-screen, Thunder Owl's wings began to glow and created a static electricity field. The field locked the enemy heroes in place. They couldn't move.

"NOW!" Tommy called to Maria.

Maria, Tommy, and Antonia unleashed their abilities. The ground shook from the Luminous Slam. Mecha-Knight shot a volley of mini-missiles. And Thunder Owl spun in another Spinning Shock. It was a triple knock-out!

THUNDER OWL

BLUE MECHA-KNIGHT

BLUE LUMINARY

ORANGE PHANTOM

ORANGE MECHA-KNIGHT

ORANGE LUMINARY

"Amazing timing Antonia!" Maria shouted.

"Sorry to keep you waiting," said Antonia.

"Okay! While they're stuck respawning, let's take out their next pillar!" said Tommy.

The trio moved swiftly across the top lane.

"Good news from the bottom lane!" came Amanda's voice. "We destroyed another pillar!"

"Great job!" Tommy responded. "Okay, change of plans. Paul, retreat and be ready to defend our bottom pillar. Amanda, hop up to the top with Maria and I. Antonia, head back to the Jungle and level up. We'll need you at your best for the last fight."

"On it!" Antonia said, directing Thunder Owl once again into the Jungle.

The next few minutes went by in a flash. After Thunder Owl's triple KO, she was two levels higher than the enemy Jungler. So when she ran into Wishing Star again, the battle was over in two quick attacks. As Wishing Star respawned slowly, Antonia cleared both sides of the Jungle. Thunder Owl had maxed out at level ten.

"One more pillar down," came Tommy's voice. "Meet up at their fifth pillar, and let's win this!"

Antonia was across the Jungle but moved swiftly to the final pillar. She was happy to have some guidance when she started out as a Jungler. But she knew that over time she would learn this too.

Finally, as she got to the edge of the forest, she could see the last pillar. An epic fight was taking place at the base. Her four teammates were locked in combat with the heroes of the Orange Earth.

With Thunder Owl hiding in the trees, Antonia waited for her abilities to recharge.

Three . . . Antonia steadied herself.

Two . . . She prepared her combo attack.

One . . . Antonia took a quick breath.

Zero! . . . Thunder Owl dashed out of the Jungle, striking and knocking out a weakened Wishing Star.

Next, Thunder Owl spun around and shot out waves of electricity hitting two more enemies.

Double KO!

Then Thunder Owl helped her team take out the remaining two enemies. As the enemies' respawn time slowly ticked along, the Blue heroes destroyed the final Orange pillar.

"We won!" Antonia shouted, leaping out of her chair.

The rest of the team followed suit. "Yes! Amazing job, everyone!" Tommy shouted. "Great first win as a new team!"

Maria came over to Antonia and held up her hand for a high five. "Thanks again for helping us earlier," Maria said.

"That's what teammates do!" Antonia said, high fiving her new teammate.

Antonia looked back at her screen and saw Thunder Owl standing in a victory pose. Her wings were outstretched and she had a wide smile on her face. The heroes of Blue Earth had prevailed! Well, at least until the next round . . .

Right, the next round, Antonia thought.

A few weeks ago, Antonia was used to playing a completely different role and different character. If she could make this much progress in just a couple of weeks, what could she do over a whole season?

"Hey, Tommy," Antonia said to her captain.

"Yeah, Antonia?"

Antonia grinned, "I'm sticking with the Jungle."

MORE ABOUT ESPORTS

- While *Mobius Bridge* is a fictional game, it was modeled after real world MOBAs such as *League of Legends*, *Dota 2*, and *Pokémon Unite*.

- Launched in 2009, *League of Legends* isn't the oldest MOBA game, but it is the most played. In 2021, *LoL* had over 180 million active users.

- MOBAs frequently add new characters to keep the game fresh for players. As of October 2021, *Dota 2* has 122 "heroes." *League of Legends* has 157 "champions." Meanwhile, the much newer *Pokémon Unite* has only about 30 playable Pokémon characters.

- Many MOBA games start with a Ban Phase. During this time, teams take turns choosing characters that cannot be used during the game. This means great players must know a few different characters in case their favorite ones are banned.

- While esports are still new in high schools, different organizations are creating new opportunities for high school students to play in various leagues and tournaments. In the summer of 2021, PlayVS held the July Jam where high school and college students competed in *Rocket League*, *League of Legends*, and *Fortnite* to win prizes totaling $40,000!

- One of the largest MOBA events each year is the *League of Legends* World Championship. In 2021, the winning team earned $489,500! Since 2011, the huge event has awarded over $30 million!

- *Dota 2*'s international tournament gives away the biggest bucks. Any player, casual or pro, who buys the *Dota 2* battle pass contributes to a huge annual prize pool. In 2021, the first place team split $18 million. Over 10 years, The international tournament has awarded over $180 million!

TALK ABOUT IT

1. Antonia is the main character in this book, and the story is told from her point of view. However, Maria also plays an important role in the story. Have you ever joined a team of people who already knew each other? What made it easy to fit in? What made it hard?

2. Tommy's role as captain meant he helped his team both inside and outside of the game. Have you had a coach or teacher who has helped you? In what ways did they help you?

3. Antonia volunteers to play a whole new role, and quickly learns she is bad at it. Have you ever signed up to try something new and didn't like it? What happened?

WRITE ABOUT IT

1. Like other MOBAs *Mobius Bridge* has dozens of heroes, but we only learn about six of them. Imagine you are a game designer and write a description of a new hero character for the game. What kind of character will it be? What role will it play? What are the hero's strengths, weaknesses, and abilities?

2. After designing a new hero, write a scene that takes place inside the world of *Mobius Bridge.* Describe how your hero uses their strengths and abilities to take out a pillar!

3. In the story we learn what Antonia, Maria, and Tommy are doing in the last game. But we don't know what happens in the bottom lane. Imagine what challenges Paul and Amanda have to overcome and write a scene from the game from one of their perspectives.

GLOSSARY

comms (KOMZ)—short for communications; a headset, microphone, or other device used to communicate with other people on a team

counter (KOUN-tuhr)—to act in opposition to someone else's action

elemental (el-uh-MEN-tuhl)—having to do with the elements of nature including earth, water, air, fire, electricity, and others

fragile (FRAJ-uhl)—easily damaged or broken

KO (KAY-OH)—stands for Knock Out; when a player is eliminated during game play

minion (MIN-yuhn)—a small or minor creature in a game that is usually weak, but often appears in large numbers

MOBA (MOH-bah)—stands for Multiplayer Online Battle Arena; a video game played on the internet, usually with multiple teammates

respawn (ree-SPAWN)—when a video game character reenters the game after having been defeated by an opposing player

scrimmage (SKRIM-ihj)—a practice game

turret (TUR-it)—a rotating structure that holds a powerful weapon used for fighting enemies in many directions

ABOUT THE AUTHOR

Daniel Mauleón grew up playing video games. Now he enjoys cheering for various esports teams including the LA Gladiators (Overwatch League) and Twolves Gaming (NBA 2kLeague).

Daniel graduated from Hamline University with a Masters in Fine Arts for Writing for Children and Young Adults in 2017. Since then, he has written a variety of books and graphic novels for kids. He lives with his wife and two cats in Minnesota.

ABOUT THE ILLUSTRATOR

Fran Bueno is a comic artist with over 25 years of experience. He graduated in Fine Arts from the Complutense University of Madrid and has worked on illustrations for pamphlets, advertisements, children's books, and young adult comics. Fran also teaches traditional inking and graphic skills at the O Garaxe Hermético Professional School of Comics. He lives in Santiago de Compostela, Spain

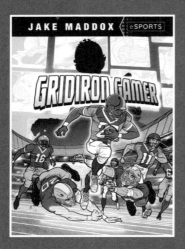